THE
MARCH WIND

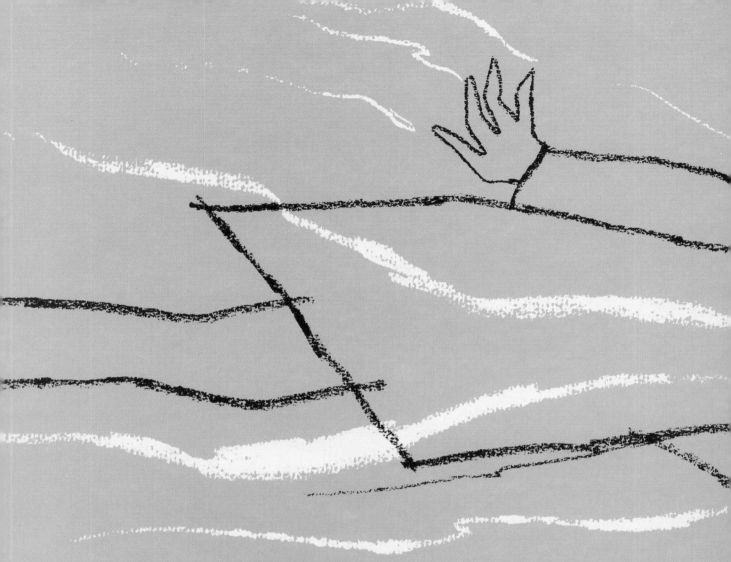

THE
MARCH WIND

INEZ RICE · ILLUSTRATED BY VLADIMIR BOBRI

So many wonderful things happen in this wonderful world of ours, yet who will believe them?
If only someone would…

The little boy picked up the hat
from the gutter. He didn't know
it was a hat at first—it looked
somewhat like a lot of other
things he had tried to pick up
that morning, only to have
the March Wind snatch them
rudely away, and hurry them off
across the street, or up into the
air. For some strange reason,
this object stayed perfectly still
as if it were trying to hide.

It was then quite a struggle for the little boy to get this particular hat on his head. Not that it was too small, but rather that there was so much water about the hat. It slopped off the brim and ran around the crown.

But, what is the use of picking up a hat if you can't put it on your head? Whatever else is there to do with a hat?

Perhaps, if you were the gentleman who lost the hat, you wouldn't understand the little boy's philosophy. Hats are supposed to be returned to owners—not worn by finders, no matter how soggy the hat or how small the finder.

How was the little boy to understand?
He had never found a hat before.
He'd never really found anything which
belonged to anybody else.

   To be sure, he'd picked up bright pebbles,
dead beetles, and even lighted fireflies.
But nobody had claimed any of these things.
In fact, nobody seemed to want them—
even as gifts.

   The little boy felt very happy with the
hat on his head. Now he could be so many
things he had always wanted to be.

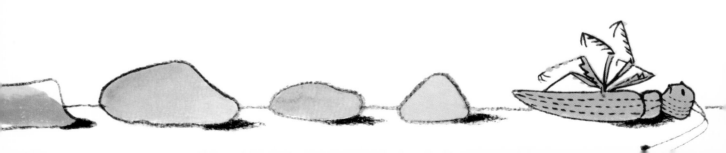

He was a soldier—
a marching soldier.
He marched straight
down the road, charging
right through puddles.
He stiffly saluted two
lamp-posts and gave an extra
long salute to the elm tree.
The tree waved its bare wet
limbs frantically in return.

He was a cowboy galloping on
a magnificent steed. He tried to
pull the ten-gallon hat from his
head and wave it majestically
to the right and to the left, but
somehow the hat felt as
heavy as if it really had ten
gallons of water in it.
And no matter how
the little boy tried,
he couldn't lift it
from his head.

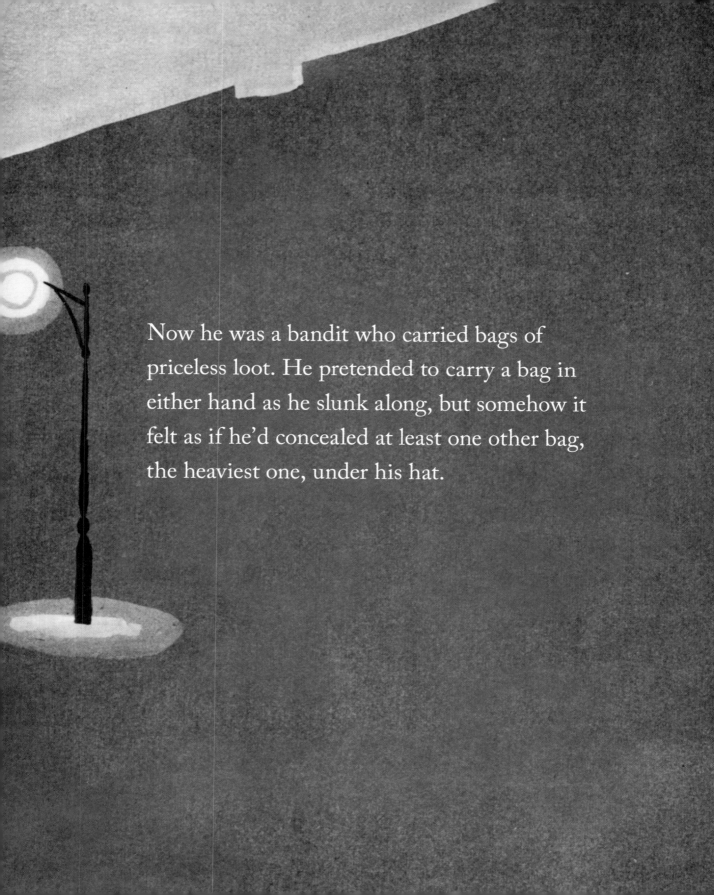

Now he was a bandit who carried bags of priceless loot. He pretended to carry a bag in either hand as he slunk along, but somehow it felt as if he'd concealed at least one other bag, the heaviest one, under his hat.

Then he turned into a stately judge who
strutted down the street in elegant grey
with a top hat to match his clothes and
his strut. People turned to stare as he
twirled his cane and his moustache. He
did not return the awestruck stares of his
townspeople. His eyes and his mind were
on loftier things. He looked high and
stumbled low, for the hat made him a little
top-heavy. But he recovered his balance.

Like magic, he became a song-and-dance man. His boots made dull splashy taps, but his songs were bright. The words didn't make much sense, yet he felt they matched the rhythm of his dancing.

He took a few low bows, but the hat never budged—not even when his head was practically upside down.

He had just finished such a sweeping bow when someone yelled, "Hey!"

It was a man—a running man with a red face and long hair streaming out behind him.

Maybe he was the one who was puffing all the wind. *Maybe* he was the March Wind himself!

The little boy was getting excited. Could he possibly say, "Hi!" to the March Wind? Just like that?

"Hi!"
The greeting didn't come from
the little boy as loudly as he had
meant it to, because the March
Wind didn't look at all friendly.
Not at all!

And he kept coming forward,
too, closer and closer.

"Where did you get that hat?"

"P... p... picked it up."

Naturally, the little boy began to be frightened. If the March Wind should accidentally blow now, when he was so close—well, where in the world would the little boy fly to? He'd be tossed about like a leaf, and how would he ever find his way home in time for supper? The next moment the hat was lifted right off the little boy's head, and for a terrible second, the little boy felt he was losing his head right along with his hat. And now, the little boy knew for a fact that this man was really the March Wind, and his knees began to tremble just as if a hurricane were flapping them back and forth.

"How did it get so wet?"

"Pu… pu… puddle!"

With the hat gone from his head, the little boy no longer felt brave as a soldier, or wild as a cowboy, or bold as a bandit, or important as a judge, or gay as a song-and-dance man.

He just felt like a little boy who is no match for the angry wind—and it was blowing now furiously through his hair and up his sleeves.

The little boy began to feel cold as
well as wind-blown. He opened his
mouth but no words came out. He
sniffled and waited silently while
the March Wind put on the hat and
stared down at him.

Then, with a queer crooked smile,
the March Wind said, almost gently,
"Well thank you for picking it up!"

And suddenly, off across the
street bounced the hat on the
head of the March Wind.

The little boy laughed to
himself. It had been a wonderful
adventure. But who would ever
believe him when he told them
he had worn the black hat of the
March Wind? Would *you*?

The Bodleian Library is home to the Iona and Peter Opie Collection of Children's Books, one of the largest and most important collections of children's books in the English language.

Published in 2017 by the Bodleian Library
Broad Street, Oxford OX1 3BG

www.bodleianshop.co.uk

ISBN: 978 1 85124 461 4

Text © Inez Rice, 1957. Illustrations © Vladimir Bobri, 1957.

First published in 1957 by Lothrop, Lee and Shepard Company, Inc. New York

Cover design by Dot Little at the Bodleian Library
Designed and typeset by 17.5 on 21 pt Tabarra Black
Printed and bound by on FSC® paper by Toppan, China on 150gsm Senbo Munk Dkal FSC®

British Library Catalogue in Publishing Data
A CIP record of this publication is available from the British Library